TO BEE, OR NOT TO BEE!

© 2023 Mojang AB. All Rights Reserved. Minecraft, the Minecraft logo, the Mojang Studios logo and the Creeper logo are trademarks of the Microsoft group of companies.

Published in the United States by Random House Children's Books, a division of Penguin Random House LLC, 1745 Broadway, New York, NY 10019, and in Canada by Penguin Random House Canada Limited, Toronto. Random House and the colophon are registered trademarks of Penguin Random House LLC.

rhcbooks.com
minecraft.net

Library of Congress Cataloging-in-Publication Data is available upon request. ISBN 978-0-593-56288-8 (trade)—ISBN 978-0-593-56289-5 (library binding)—ISBN 978-0-593-56290-1 (ebook)

Cover design by Diane Choi

Printed in the United States of America

2nd Printing

TO BEE, OR NOT TO BEE!

By Nick Eliopulos
Illustrated by Alan Batson and Chris Hill

Random House New York

MORGAN

ASH

HARPER

PO

JODI

THEO

Prologue

Harper didn't want to hurt the bees.

They weren't making it easy for her, though.

They were buzzing all around her. One of them broke loose from the swarm, diving at her. It aimed its stinger right at her face.

She lifted her shield just in time, batting it away. But she knew it would try again.

A hissing sounded at her back. **She spun around as a spider lunged at her.**

"Bad spider!" she said, swatting at it with her empty hand. That knocked it back, giving her some room. Maybe she could escape. . . .

But more buzzing forced her to whirl around

again. Another bee struck her shield.

And then another.

And another.

The spider hissed behind her. **She could sense its approach.**

She turned . . .

And again . . .

And again . . .

She couldn't keep this up for long.

It was a battle of the bugs. And both sides wanted to destroy her.

And the worst part was this: if she fought back, she and her friends—and maybe the entire Overworld—were **doomed.**

Chapter 1

TO BEE, OR NOT TO BEE MARKED ABSENT IS NOT A GOOD QUESTION TO ASK THIS EARLY IN THE MORNING.

Woodsword Middle School was abuzz with excitement.

Harper Houston had never really understood that expression before today. But as she stood on the front lawn of the school, surrounded by her classmates, she could hear it. **It was the sound of dozens of students whispering at once.** Their voices were too low—and too numerous—for Harper to make out any individual words. But those voices, overlapping and reverberating across the lawn?

Together, they sounded distinctly like a *buzz*.

Harper's entire grade had been instructed to

meet their homeroom group on the lawn. Now her homeroom teacher, Ms. Minerva, was attempting to take attendance while a hundred kids chattered and squirmed with excitement. She seemed a little flustered. **Her hair was extra frizzy, and her eyes were a little intense.** She took a long sip of her coffee, followed by a deep breath.

"Theo?" she said, raising her voice to be heard over the racket. **"Is Theo Grayson here?"**

"Present!" said Theo, and he cut through the crowd, waving his hand in the air. "I wasn't late, honest! I just got a little lost."

Ms. Minerva checked off his name on her clipboard. "Harper Houston?" she said.

"Here," said Harper, then turned to greet Theo.

"What's going on?" Theo asked her. **"This is highly unusual ... even for Woodsword."**

"Nobody knows for sure," said Harper. "But I'm pretty sure I heard Ms. Minerva muttering under her breath about how this is all Doc's fault."

"Oh no," said Morgan Mercado. He cradled the class hamster, **Baron Sweetcheeks**, against his chest. "If Doc's involved, it could be almost anything. She didn't try to replace the lunch ladies with robots again, did she? It took weeks to clean all the Sloppy Joes off the ceiling. . . ."

Po Chen chuckled. "That's nothing," he said. "Remember when the computer lab became a butterfly sanctuary? Maybe the whole school has become an iguana habitat!"

Jodi Mercado, Morgan's little sister, pressed her hands together with delight. "That actually sounds adorable," she said. She loved animals of all kinds.

"I know, right?" Po laughed again. "Iguanas need an education, too!"

Harper grinned. **She was fairly certain that the school hadn't been taken over by reptiles or robots.** But her friends were right about one thing. Doc—their nickname for Dr. Culpepper, their science teacher—could be unpredictable. Harper didn't mind. In fact, she looked up to Doc.

A loud horn sounded, interrupting Harper's thoughts and nearly jolting her out of her skin. She looked up—along with every other person on the lawn—and saw a pick-up truck rounding the corner. It pulled to a stop at the curb, blocking their view of the library across the street. And driving the truck . . . was **Doc Culpepper** herself.

The science teacher honked twice more, and the kids broke into cheers. There was something strange and delightful about seeing their teacher at the wheel of the big vehicle.

Doc hopped out of the cab, joined by a man who

had been sitting beside her in the passenger seat. **The man had white hair and wrinkles around his eyes, and he wore cowboy boots.** Harper guessed that he was the owner of the truck.

But what was the truck hauling? The back was covered with a massive tarp, making its contents a mystery.

"What do you think is in there?" Harper asked.

"Iguanas... or puppies," said Jodi hopefully.

"Robot custodians," suggested Morgan.

"Alien spaceships!" Po guessed.

"It could be anything," said Theo. Then he thought about it. "Probably not spaceships."

"Bonjour, mes étudiants!" Doc said, speaking through a high-tech bullhorn. She laughed, pressing a button. "Oops. I had it on the wrong setting. Let's try that again. Good morning, students!"

The buzzing of the crowd stopped as voices rang out in unison: "Good morning!"

"I'd like to introduce a friend of mine," said Doc. She gestured to the man standing beside her. "This is Mr. Shane. He has a very interesting job—one that takes him all over the country. For the next few weeks, he'll be right here in our hometown. And he's brought a few thousand of his closest friends." Doc winked at the man. "Whenever you're ready, Mr. Shane."

Mr. Shane gripped a corner of the tarp, and he pulled. The tarp fell away, revealing stacks of crates, **all of them swarming with insects.** They flew into the air, buzzing around the truck, immediately taking the opportunity to explore the area.

"**Bees!**" said Harper. She'd never seen so many bees in all her life.

"Mr. Shane is a bee wrangler—or an apiarist, if you want to use the scientific term," Doc said into her bullhorn. "His truck is loaded with beehives, and he brings the hives—and the honeybees who live in them—wherever they're needed."

"Wherever they're *needed*?" Morgan said to his friends. "Aren't they pests?"

"I don't know," said Jodi. "**I love animals. But stinging insects aren't exactly cuddly.**"

"And they follow an outdated form of government," Po said, motioning dramatically toward the truck. "Down with the monarchy! We're a democratic republic in *this* country, honeybees."

Theo shushed them. "I'm trying to listen!" he said.

Harper nodded at him, grateful. She wanted to hear what Doc had to say, too.

"I can tell you all have questions," said Doc. "And that's a good thing! **We'll be talking more about bees all week in science class.**" She handed the bullhorn to Mr. Shane.

"**Bees are fascinating creatures,**" he said. "And they're important to the ecosystem. I've spent my life learning about them. And I *still* learn something new, most days."

"Mr. Shane has to drive his truck over to the town orchard this morning," said Doc. "But he's agreed to leave one hive behind for a few days. We'll keep it on library property, right across from the school, where we can keep an eye on it—and maybe learn a thing or two ourselves." She placed a hand on the man's shoulder. "Let's all make a

promise to Mr. Shane. Let's promise we'll take care of the insects he's entrusting to us. Promise?"

"Promise!" Harper called, along with many of the other students.

But after she'd said it, she felt a little anxious. How did a person take care of insects, exactly? How could she keep them safe from harm?

Harper had a sinking feeling it might be harder than it sounded.

Chapter 2

THE SECRET TO SUCCESSFUL ANIMAL FRIENDSHIPS? LOTS OF SNACKS!

"**I** think we need to talk about the giant hole in the sky," said Harper.

They were in Minecraft—not just playing the game, but inside it. Together, Harper and her friends were experiencing a hyper-real simulation that they could only access with special Doc-enhanced VR goggles. It never ceased to amaze Harper that they were in the world of Minecraft. Thanks to Doc's mad science, their favorite game had come to life!

But now, she feared that something was very wrong with that world.

"Do we have to focus on the negatives?"

complained Po. "I'm moooo-dy enough as it is."

Po liked to wear different skins to express himself. Today, he was in a mooshroom skin, in honor of their recent temporary teammate, a mushroom-covered cow named Michael G. "I really miss that guy," Po said.

"He was an excellent addition to the team," Jodi agreed. "But he's safer not following us around. **WE TEND TO GET INTO A LOT OF FIGHTS.**"

"And talking about the Fault isn't 'focusing on the negatives,'" Morgan argued. "If we're going to find a solution, we have to acknowledge the problem."

"What we really need to do is find the Evoker King," said Theo. **"OR THE 'EVOKER SPAWN,' I GUESS. AT LEAST, THAT'S WHAT I'M CALLING THE PIECES HE BROKE INTO."** He gazed worriedly at the rift overhead. "Finding them is our best hope of bringing this place back from the brink of disaster."

Harper figured Theo knew what he was talking about. As the group's only programmer, he'd spent some time studying the computer code at the heart of the game. It was Theo who had figured out what happened to their former enemy turned friend, the Evoker King, an artificial intelligence who had lived inside this version of Minecraft. **The Evoker King's very essence had been split into six distinct pieces.** Those pieces had taken the form of unusual mobs. So far, Harper and her friends had confronted three of those mobs. They had been successful in retrieving half of the Evoker King's code.

They needed three more pieces to save the Evoker King . . . to put him back together again and stop the rest of the program from breaking down entirely.

The sixth member of their team, Ash Kapoor, had joined them for the day's scouting mission. Ash lived in a different town, **but distance didn't matter in this virtual world.** Harper felt as if she were truly standing right beside Ash. She reached out and put her arm around Ash's shoulder. Even though she was only touching an avatar, it felt solid to the touch.

"I'm glad you're here," Harper told her. "An extra set of eyes could come in handy."

"It can't hurt, right?" said Ash. "Especially when we're looking for something as small as a butterfly."

Butterflies weren't a normally occurring Minecraft mob, and they only showed up whenever one of the Evoker Spawn was near. They were like digital ghosts, virtual echoes of the Evoker King's metamorphosis.

They were *clues.* And Harper knew they desperately needed clues.

Suddenly, she saw a flash of movement out of the corner of her eye. Not a butterfly—it was a rabbit, darting across the grass.

Po screamed. **"LOOK OUT!"** he said.

Harper gave him a funny look. "It's just a rabbit," she said.

"Am I the only one who remembers that time we were attacked by rabbits?" he asked. "I still see their beady little eyes in the dark when I'm trying to get to sleep."

"Those rabbits were being mind-controlled by a giant cave spider with self-esteem issues," Theo reminded him.

"That doesn't make it any less weird," said Po. "Or more forgettable . . ."

"Oh, cute!" said Jodi. "Look. The bunny has a friend."

Harper looked where Jodi was pointing. **A fox hurried past them, heading the**

same way the rabbit had gone.

"HE WENT THAT WAY!" Jodi told the fox. "If you hurry, you should be able to catch him." She sighed, then turned to her friends. "I love animal friendships. I have a whole notebook full of cute animal photos I found online."

"Uh, Jodi," said Morgan. "You realize—"

Ash cleared her throat, cutting Morgan off. She shook her head at him, signaling that he shouldn't say what he was about to say.

"What?" said Jodi. "What is it?"

"NEVER MIND," Morgan said. "Don't worry about it."

Harper knew what Morgan was thinking. She knew he was a good big brother—too kind and protective to upset Jodi unnecessarily.

Harper *also* also knew that Theo was not as careful with other people's feelings.

"They aren't friends," said Theo. "The fox is going to catch and eat the rabbit."

Harper was reasonably sure that avatars couldn't blush or blanch. **Yet Jodi's blocky face appeared suddenly pale.** Her mouth

dropped open. "What?" said Jodi. "That's awful!"

"No, it isn't," said Theo. **"IT'S JUST NATURE."**

"Nature or not," said Po, "I'm rooting for the rabbit. Run, little guy! All is forgiven!"

"Can't we do something to help?" asked Jodi.

"That's a kind thought," said Harper.

"But it's pointless," said Theo. "You shouldn't try to disrupt the food web. Even if you *could,* it would be a disaster."

Harper sighed, turning to Jodi. "Theo is a little blunt," she said. "But he isn't wrong. We learned all about this in science class, remember? **HERBIVORES, LIKE RABBITS, EAT GRASS. CARNIVORES, LIKE FOXES, EAT OTHER**

ANIMALS. If you saved all the rabbits, the foxes would starve. And there wouldn't be enough grass to feed the rabbits."

"It's all part of the circle of life," Ash said, agreeing with Harper. "The Minecraft fox is programmed to act like a real-world fox. **IT ISN'T EVIL OR MEAN . . . IT'S JUST DOING WHAT IT NEEDS TO DO TO SURVIVE.**"

Morgan put his arm around Jodi's shoulders. "Don't worry," he said. "The rabbit might get away! And if it doesn't, there are a lot more rabbits out there. We'll see another one soon, I bet."

"MAYBE THAT BUTTERFLY WILL LEAD US TO ONE," said Po.

"Sure," said Morgan. "That's something I love about this game. You never know what you're going to— Wait." His head snapped up. "What butterfly?"

Po grinned, pointing. **A luminous, pixelated insect fluttered nearby.**

"FOLLOW IT," said Theo and Morgan simultaneously.

"It's surely what Michael G. would have wanted," Po added.

Chapter 3

CALLING LIGHTNING DOWN FROM A MYSTERIOUS RIP IN THE SKY . . . AND OTHER QUESTIONABLE IDEAS

Jodi tried not to think about the rabbit. Had it gotten away? **Or had the fox caught it in the end?**

She would never know. But she *could* learn where the butterflies were leading them.

"Focus on the butterflies," she said to herself.

There had been only one of them at first. But as it led them across the taiga biome, **OTHER BUTTERFLIES HAD JOINED IT.** Now there were four of them, flittering around each other. Fortunately, they were all moving in the same direction.

"I bet if a parrot swooped down and started

eating those butterflies, you'd try to stop it," she said to her brother.

"I don't know," said Morgan. "It might be interesting to see what would happen. Any theories?"

Theo tapped his chin. "If the butterflies are stray bits of the Evoker King's code . . . maybe the parrot would be transformed by eating them?"

"THE EVOKER PARROT!" said Ash. "Sounds cute."

"I agree," said Po. "Maybe if I wore my pirate skin, he'd hang out on my shoulder."

The kids laughed. Then lightning crackled

from the Fault overhead and the sound of thunder made them jump! All at once, they remembered what was at stake.

Jodi knew they were entering a new biome when the trees changed. There had been nothing but spruce trees in the taiga biome. Now they were walking among a cluster of oak and birch trees.

Jodi wasn't a plant person, really. But she knew her Minecraft trees. They all provided wood of different colors, and that was important to know when planning a colorful build.

For the same reason, she was trying to learn all the flowers of Minecraft. But there were so many different types! Some of them could be used to make dyes, but not all of them. And usually, they were spread across an assortment of different biomes.

But as Jodi stepped past the trees, she saw a huge array of flowers growing on the gentle slopes ahead. It was like a rainbow had come down to nestle in the grass.

"WHAT IS THIS PLACE?" she asked in awe.

"IT LOOKS LIKE A FLOWER FOREST BIOME," said Theo. "Almost every kind of flower grows here."

"Could the butterflies be attracted to the flowers?" asked Harper.

"I don't know," said Ash, pointing with her blocky hand. "They seem more interested in *that*."

Jodi saw what Ash meant. The butterflies had all gathered around a block that was hanging from a nearby oak tree. The block was yellow with bands of brown. Small openings in its sides made it look almost like a miniature house.

"IT'S A BEES' NEST!" said Morgan.

"Why are the butterflies gathered around it?" Harper asked.

"Do you think the next Evoker Spawn could be **A GIANT BEE?"** asked Ash.

But Jodi wasn't paying attention. She'd spotted a sheep grazing among the flowers. Pressing herself again a nearby birch, she scanned the area for wolves and other predators. For now, the sheep appeared safe. But how long would that last?

"Psst," Jodi whispered. "Hey, Po."

While the others were gathered around the bees' nest, Jodi pulled Po aside. "Do you still have that trident?" she asked him.

Po gave her a suspicious look. "Yeeeah," he said, and **he glanced up at the lightning that flashed around the edges of the Fault.** "What do you need it for?"

"I had an idea," Jodi said. "Your trident has a special enchantment on it, right? It causes lightning to strike."

"When it's raining, sure," said Po. He looked

up again at the Fault. "You think it'll work on the lightning that's flashing around the Fault?"

"I THINK IT MIGHT WORK," Jodi said.

"Okay," said Po. "But why do you *want* to call lightning down?"

Jodi looked around to make sure her brother couldn't hear her, and then she fixed Po with her most serious expression. She asked him, "Do you remember what happened when a pig got struck by lightning?"

Po nodded. **"UH, YEAH! THE PIG WAS TRANSFORMED INTO A MONSTROUS, UNDEAD MOB PIG-HUMAN HYBRID THINGY."**

He shuddered. "It's not the sort of thing a person forgets."

"Do you think it

would work on other animals, too?" asked Jodi. "Like that sheep over there?"

"Jodi," said Po, and he put his blocky hands on her shoulders. **"YOU KNOW I LOVE A GOOD BAD IDEA.** But why would you want to transform another animal into a monstrous, undead hybrid? Are you worried that Piggy Sue is out there somewhere, terribly lonely?"

"I'll bet Piggy Sue doesn't have to worry about being eaten by predators," said Jodi. **"IF WE CAN TRANSFORM THAT SHEEP, THEN IT'LL BE SAFE, TOO."**

Po thought about it for a minute. "Yeah," he said at last. "I support this idea one hundred percent. It's unusual. Which I *always* mean as a compliment." He handed her the trident. "Want to do the honors? You'll have to throw it at the sheep."

Jodi hesitated. "You don't think anything bad will happen? **THE LIGHTNING FROM THE FAULT IS PROBABLY JUST LIKE NORMAL LIGHTNING, RIGHT?"**

Po rubbed his square jaw for a moment, and

then said, "It will be fine. **WHAT'S THE WORST THAT COULD HAPPEN?"**

Jodi smiled, gave Po a fist bump, then turned and crept toward the sheep. **The animal looked up from its grazing,** and Jodi waved. Then it went back to what it was doing, obviously deciding that she wasn't a threat.

"Good choice," said Jodi. "I'm here to help, after all."

Just as she took aim with the trident, Po said, "Um—but I just remembered that this will kill the sheep."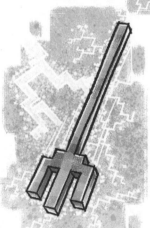

"WHAT?!" Jodi yelled as she let go of the trident. Luckily her shock caused her to throw the trident into the air and way off course.

Lightning from the Fault leapt out at the trident, causing a massive flash. Hot sparks showered down from the sky. **NEARBY TREES AND BRUSH BEGAN TO SMOLDER AS THE SPARKS HIT. THE SHEEP RAN AWAY.**

Po and Jodi looked at each other. Po said, "I think the sheep has the right idea. Let's go."

The two friends took off through the trees hoping to find their friends—and hoping nothing too bad would come from the sparks caused by their failed experiment. Jodi soon heard a strange sound. **She looked up and saw that the tree contained another bees' nest.** And it was buzzing with activity.

"Something's happening!" said Morgan. "Jodi? Po?"

"We're over here!" said Jodi, and she grabbed Po and pulled him toward the others.

THERE WAS A BUZZING COMING FROM BEHIND THEM. AND TO THE SIDE. AND UP AHEAD . . .

They were surrounded by the sound of buzzing insects.

"What's happening?" Po asked as their friends came into view.

"MORGAN DISTURBED THE BEES," said Theo.

"I did not!" said Morgan. **"I ONLY POKED**

THE NEST A LITTLE BIT."

"It's so loud!" said Harper, covering her ears.

"I hate to say this," said Ash, "but we should be ready for a fight. Just in case . . ."

As Ash drew her sword, the first bee appeared. It floated out from the first nest they'd found, wings beating furiously.

Jodi wasn't always fond of insects. But this insect was decidedly cute, with big eyes and itty-bitty antennae sticking out from its head. "Oh!" she said. "I don't want to fight it."

"It's okay," said Morgan, and he put his hand on Ash's sword. "It isn't hostile right now."

"How can you tell?" she asked.

Morgan frowned. "BELIEVE ME. IF IT WERE HOSTILE, YOU'D KNOW."

Two more bees appeared from the first nest. They flew into the air, joining their hive mate. And they weren't alone. More bees approached, flying in from all over the forest. There must have been a dozen nests nearby, and now all those bees were coming together in a great, billowing swarm.

The buzzing grew in intensity as dozens of wings vibrated at the same time.

"Fascinating," said Harper. "It almost looks like they're dancing in the air."

As Jodi watched, the insects spun and swirled in a great mass. They sped up, moving so fast that their wings and bodies blurred, and the buzzing grew louder than ever. And then, to Jodi's astonishment . . . the bees made a shape.

It was the shape of a *human*. Some of the bees lined up like limbs. Others clumped together to form a torso. And the head . . .

The head appeared to be looking right at them.

"That's . . . new," said Morgan.

"Shh!" said Ash. "Do you hear that?"

Jodi strained to catch the sounds. But all she heard was **the buzzing.**

And then she realized that the buzzing almost sounded like a word, repeated over and over: *Lzzn. Lzzn.*

Listen.

As Jodi watched, the bees' wings began to move in perfect unison. The pitch of the buzzing changed as their wings went faster or slower.

The bees were trying to tell them something.

"*Lizzzzen,*" they said. "*Youuu . . . muzzzzt . . .*"

It was then that a great bolt of lightning struck a nearby tree.

Jodi gasped in surprise.

The bees broke apart, each one flying away in a different direction.

And nearby . . . **a fire began to rapidly spread through the forest.**

Chapter 4

EXCUSE ME, FELLOW MINECRAFT PLAYERS, WE DON'T WANT TO ALARM YOU, BUT FIRE!!!

As he watched the flames spread through the forest biome, **Theo froze with inaction.**

Fire was dangerous and destructive. No one would blame Theo for being afraid.

But Theo *wasn't* afraid. He was too busy feeling annoyed.

"Everyone, get clear," said Morgan. "And don't panic! We can retreat to the taiga biome. **WE'LL COME BACK WHEN IT'S SAFE.**"

"No!" said Theo. "It might be too late by then."

"Too late?" said Ash. "What do you mean?"

"THOSE BEES," said Theo. **"THEY WERE**

TRYING TO COMMUNICATE WITH US. They were trying to tell us something. And now . . . Oh no!"

Theo's heart sank as he saw it happen. Fire had spread to a nearby oak tree . . . destroying one of the bees' nests in a matter of seconds.

"We have to do something," said Theo. **"WE HAVE TO GIVE THE BEES ANOTHER CHANCE TO DELIVER THEIR MESSAGE."**

"I see what Theo means," said Harper. "If the bees are destroyed, we might lose our chance to fix the Evoker King."

"It would also be bad for the bees," said Jodi. "I'm sure they would love to not be destroyed today."

"Okay," said Ash. "New plan. **STOP THE**

FIRE! SAVE THE BEES!"

They scattered, each doing their best to stop flames from spreading.

Morgan and Ash ran to a nearby stream and filled their buckets with water. **"DO YOU THINK THIS WILL MAKE A DIFFERENCE?"** asked Ash.

"It will if we use this water to set up a whole new water source," said Morgan. "We could actually create a river in the heart of the forest."

"Sounds like a plan," said Ash.

"I'LL DIG SOME CANALS," offered Harper, and she pulled out her shovel. "Even if we don't fill them with water, the gaps should stop the fire from spreading across the grass."

As Harper started carving lines through the landscape, Theo finally sprang into action. He followed close behind Harper, grabbing the dirt blocks that she left in her wake. "I can use these to make walls of dirt. **THEY'LL BE LIKE**

BARRIERS AGAINST THE FLAMES."

"DON'T TRAP THE ANIMALS!" said Jodi. She ran ahead of Harper and Theo, moving toward the heart of the forest with a sheaf of wheat in her hand. "If they get stuck behind your canals or your walls of dirt, they'll be in a lot of danger!"

"I'd better get the trident we left behind," said Po. "The last thing we need is a second lightning strike."

Theo stopped. "TRIDENT?" he echoed. "Po, did you cause this fire?"

"Busy now," said Po as he rushed past them. "Talk later!"

Jodi emerged from between the trees, leading a sheep to safety. "IT'S MY FAULT," she said. "I put the trident down and then forgot about it. I'm really sorry."

"Tell that to the bees," Theo said. As he watched, another nest fell into the flames.

"WE HAVE TO GET THOSE NESTS OUT OF HERE," said Theo. "We're losing too many of them."

"There's a nest right over there." Harper pointed at a nearby tree with her shovel. "Should I cut it out of the tree?" she asked.

"Wait!" said Morgan. "If you use that, you'll just destroy it."

"We need a pickaxe with a Silk Touch enchantment," said Ash, and she ran to Harper's side. **"I HAVE SOME LAPIS.** Do you have an enchanting table?"

Harper nodded, placing the workstation down beside the tree. On either side of the enchanting table, she set down bookcases. "I'm going to need a minute," she said. "Someone keep an eye on the fire, please."

"I've got your back," said Theo, and he placed a dirt barrier all around the tree—and around Harper, who was now free to work without fear of the flames reaching her.

The pickaxe she was working on glowed purple with magic, but Harper shook her head. "That didn't work right," she said. "It's a Fortune enchantment."

"KEEP TRYING," said Theo, and he handed her a spare pickaxe. "You'll get the right enchantment eventually." He just hoped it happened before they ran out of materials in their inventory.

"THAT DID IT!" Harper said after the third try. She lifted the glowing tool from the enchanting table and tossed it to Ash, who was closest to the nest.

Ash smiled, and her new pickaxe seemed to glow more brightly as it swung through the air, cutting the bees' nest loose from the tree.

Harper caught the nest and carried it to safety.

Theo hoped that would be enough. He hoped the bee being wasn't lost to them forever.

But as he looked over the smoldering ruins of the forest . . . beneath the growing wound in the sky . . .

He found it hard to be very hopeful at all.

Chapter 5

FLIGHT OF THE HONEYBEE. FRIGHT OF THE STUDENTS. A CHANCE TO JOIN THE DANCE!

The next day in science class, Po was still feeling guilty. He had known the trident wasn't a toy. And he really, really should have realized that leaving it in the middle of a forest was a bad idea.

"You didn't do it on purpose," Morgan said. "Don't be so hard on yourself."

"And that goes double for me," said Jodi. "Right?"

"*You* should have known better," said Morgan. "I mean, a mutant sheep beast? Even if that was possible, why would you want to see it?"

"A sheep beast would have been able to protect itself from wolves. It might have protected other sheep, too," said Jodi. Morgan raised an eyebrow. "Well, it *seemed* like a good idea at the time!"

"It really did," said Po. **"Your sister can be very convincing."**

Class hadn't started yet, and Po was just pulling out his textbook when Harper slumped into a nearby seat.

"Everything okay?" asked Morgan.

"I was up late reading about bees," answered Harper. "I wanted to get a head start on today's lesson."

Po nodded sagely. "Yeah, doing extra homework would bum me out, too."

"No, you don't understand," said Harper. "I ended up reading about something called *colony collapse disorder.* It's when an entire colony of bees just . . . dies. Scientists don't totally understand why, but it's happening a lot." **She dropped her head on the desk.** "You know how I get when I start worrying about the environment."

"Man," said Morgan. **"Everyone has a lot of feelings today, huh?"**

"Bees," Doc said so suddenly and so forcefully that Po jolted to attention. "They are marvels of nature. Without them, we would have no fruits! No flowers! And . . . no honey!"

Po gasped. **"But . . . but my mom puts honey in her peanut butter and honey sandwiches.** It's a key ingredient!"

"You have the humble honeybee to thank for your sandwiches, Po," said Doc. She thought about it for moment. "You should also thank your mother. Honestly, you're probably old enough to be making your own sandwiches."

Po gasped again.

Their classmate, Shelly Silver, raised her hand. "But *why* do bees make honey?" she asked. "They aren't just doing it to be nice, are they?"

"No indeed," said Doc. "Bees make honey so that they'll have something to eat during the winter, when there are no flowers in bloom. Typically, a bee's diet consists of nectar. That's why you'll see them buzzing around flowers so often."

Theo entered the classroom late, which was unusual for him. "I'm so sorry, Doc," he said. "I was with Ms. Minerva. She . . . uh, she wanted me to read this note to you."

"Go ahead," said Doc.

Theo cleared his throat, then read aloud from

a sheet of paper. "Dear Doc, Please excuse Theo's tardiness to science class. **He is a member of our school's newest extracurricular club, the Woodsword Gardening and Landscaping Club.** We have our work cut out for us ever since *someone* thought it would be a good idea to have a hundred students all trample the front yard. Sincerely, Ms. Minerva." Theo grinned bashfully. "And she drew a little smiley face. But it sort of looks like it's scowling. . . ."

"Thank you for your service to our school, Theo," said Doc. "Please have a seat, and I'll compose a reply for you to take back to Minerva. Honestly, if she'd just used my combination lawn mower, woodchipper, and hedge trimmer, the yard would be in fine shape by now. 'Too many blades,' she said."

Theo slipped into his seat, obviously less than enthusiastic about running notes back and forth between the teachers.

Po gave him a little pat on the back and a sympathetic smile.

"The problem here is that Minerva is a bit of a queen bee . . . and so am I," said Doc. "A bee colony has only one queen—no more and no less."

"What other sorts of bees are there?" asked Morgan. **"King bees? Royal vizier bees?" "Court jester bees?"** asked Po.

Doc shook her head. "Aside from the queen, every adult bee in the colony is either a drone or a worker. The drones are male bees. They have no stinger, and they stay behind to tend to the queen. But the workers, ah! The workers are female bees, and they go out and explore the world."

As if Doc had somehow summoned it, a bee flew in through the open window. The teacher smiled, obviously happy to have a visitor.

"It's a bee!" cried Morgan.

"Look out, here it comes!" yelled Po.

Someone screamed, and then half the kids in class were on their feet, ducking and dodging to stay out of the bee's path.

"Students, students!" said Doc. She held up her hands to signal for calm. **"There's no reason to panic."**

"Sure there is," said Po, and he kept his eyes on the bee as he spoke. "Bees use their stingers to inject venom. The venom can cause pain, irritation, and even an allergic reaction."

"Aw," said Harper. "You *did* do the homework."

"A bee uses its stinger to defend its hive and its queen," said Doc. "They aren't aggressive, and they won't attack unless you give them a reason to."

"So we should all just stay calm," said Harper. **She walked toward the bee and, with a sheet of paper, guided the insect back out the window.**

"Well!" said Doc. "That was one

worker bee who had a little adventure. She didn't find any nectar in here, so she'll keep looking."

"What will the worker bee do when she finds nectar?" asked Jodi. "Imagine she finds a garden that's full of flowers—full of food! She can't bring it all back by herself, can she?"

"No, she cannot. She'll need help," said Doc. "Where do you think she'll find it? What would *you* do?"

"I would go back to my hive," said Po. "I'd want to tell all the other worker bees about the garden. Then they could help me bring back all the nectar."

"But how are you going to do that, Po?" said Doc. **"You're a bee! You can't talk."**

"Oh," said Po. "Uh . . . could I point?"

"You're not far off," said Doc. "When a honeybee wants to communicate with the hive . . . they communicate with movement. Through a complicated series of gestures, they can relay information about where to find a food source, as well as the quality and quantity of the food there."

Jodi couldn't help imagining—**because**

her imagination was always a little wild—Doc dancing with a human-sized bee at a fancy party. They looked so elegant as they danced around and around.

"I'm sorry," said Po. "But are you saying . . . that bees *dance* to communicate?"

"That's what I'm saying," confirmed Doc.

Po's jaw dropped. He could feel his eyes go wide.

"I want to be more like a bee," he said. "Less talk! More rhythmic movement." Po performed a bold interpretive dance with his arms, making full use of his wrists and fingers. It looked like he was weaving spells in the air. Jodi joined in, waving her hands above her head.

"This dance is communicating . . . that

Harper should cheer up!" said Jodi.

Harper laughed. "Well, it's working!"

"I think Jodi and Po have the right idea," said Doc. "Come on, class. Let's all be a little more . . . bee."

The class cheered. Some of them stood. Some stayed seated. **But they all danced to their own imagined beat.**

And Po couldn't help feeling like he had the very best colony a kid could ask for.

Chapter 6

IN A WORLD OF EMAILS, TEXTS, AND POP-UP ADS, THE MESSAGE HAS BEEN RECEIVED . . . SORT OF.

Harper laughed when she saw Po's new Minecraft skin.

"Do you like *thizzz?*" he said.

"Very much," said Harper. "In fact, I'd say that outfit is very *bee*-coming."

Po, naturally, had found a bee skin. It was yellow with brown stripes, with short antennae sticking out from the head and a couple of wings in the back.

"Do the wings work?" asked Jodi.

"I wish," said Po. "But no. They're just for show."

"IT'S TOO BAD WE DON'T HAVE ANY ELYTRA WINGS," said Morgan. "Then you'd be able to fly. Or glide, at least."

"You know, I might be able to do something about that," said Theo. "I could import some elytra into this version of the game from my home computer."

"Maybe not until we've solved that," said Morgan, and he pointed up at the Fault. **"I DON'T THINK WE SHOULD BE MESSING WITH THE CODE RIGHT NOW. WE COULD MAKE THINGS WORSE."**

"We sort of did make things worse," said Jodi, and she gazed miserably out at the ruined forest. Most of the trees and flowers had burned away entirely. **"I FEEL ROTTEN ABOUT CAUSING SO MUCH DAMAGE."**

"Me too," said Po. "I think we should stay here for a little while. Maybe we can repair the forest."

"No way!" said Theo. "The butterflies—the

mission! That's all that matters."

"Aren't you in the landscaping club?" said Po. **"I'D SAY THIS AREA NEEDS SOME LANDSCAPING."**

"That's in real life," said Theo. "The flower forest isn't a real place with real plants, remember? It's just programmed to appear that way. It doesn't really matter if it looks nice or not."

"I'm with Theo," said Morgan. "The fire was a huge distraction. We need to get back to our mission."

"MAYBE THIS IS THE MISSION," said Jodi. "Maybe we need to fix our mistake."

"*That* is what we need to fix," said Morgan, pointing to the Fault again. "We're clearly running out of time."

"Ash would agree with Po and me, I bet," said Jodi.

"Ash isn't here today," said Morgan. **"SHE HAD A SCOUT MEETING AT HER NEW SCHOOL."** He turned to Harper. "So it's up to Harper to cast the deciding vote."

Harper squirmed a little. She didn't enjoy being

the decision maker for the entire group. And she could see both points of view so clearly!

But it felt wrong to leave such damage and destruction in their wake. "What's a flower forest biome without flowers and trees?" she said. **"We can fix this place up a little and keep an eye out for bees and butterflies at the same time.** As a matter of fact . . ." From her inventory, Harper pulled out the nest they'd saved.

"I'd forgotten that!" said Theo.

"I've been studying it," said Harper. "I think there are bees inside, but they won't come out while I'm holding it. SO THE FIRST STEP OF OUR FOREST RESTORATION PROJECT CAN BE FINDING A NEW TREE FOR THIS NEST."

"That feels like a good compromise," said Morgan.

"I actually have some flowers in my inventory," said Jodi. "I was going to use them to make dyes, but I could replant them here instead."

"And I've got a couple saplings," said Theo, holding up a small tree. "I picked them up when

I was gathering wood recently. I bet we could get some more in a nearby biome."

"*Buzz buzz,*" said Po. "I like *thizz* plan!"

They got to work. And Harper found herself having fun. When they'd reacted to the fire, they had all tried different tactics. The energy had been frantic, and they'd all panicked a little. But now they were working together as a team.

They discussed where to put each flower. **"THESE DANDELIONS LOOK SO HAPPY IN THIS PATCH OF SUNLIGHT,"** said Jodi.

They worked out the best place to plant saplings. "If we put four of them together like this, they'll grow into a single big tree," said Morgan.

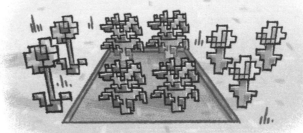

They all looked for the perfect spot to leave the bees' nest. "That oak tree looks *juzzt* right," said Po, pointing.

Harper did the honors. She climbed a staircase of dirt and placed the nest high in the tree. Almost as soon as she did so, it buzzed with activity.

"It's working," said Harper, hopping back down the staircase. "Here they come!"

Three bees emerged from the nest.

They spread out in the air around the tree.

"I think they approve of their new home," said Jodi with delight.

"But will they swarm together again?" asked Morgan. "Will they form a shape and finish what they were saying before?"

Harper shook her head. "Three bees aren't enough. I don't hear any more buzzing out there." She frowned. **"I THINK**

THESE ARE THE ONLY BEES TO SURVIVE
THE FIRE."

"And they look . . . glitched," said Theo. He couldn't keep the disappointment from his voice. "Look. They're just making the same movements over and over again."

Theo was right. Each bee was making a different motion, seemingly caught in a type of loop. "That one's just moving in circles," said Harper.

"Movement," said Po. Then his eyes lit up beneath his antennae. "What if the movements mean something?" he said. "Just like in real life. THEY COULD BE TRYING TO COMMUNICATE WITH MOTION!"

The bees suddenly buzzed in unison, as if in agreement.

"Is the circle supposed to be a zero?" asked Theo.

"Or the letter *O*!" said Jodi. "Because this one looks like it's making a capital *P*."

"Aw, you guys," said Po. "THEY'RE SPELLING MY NAME!"

Harper laughed. "I think it's a coincidence.

Because the third bee is making the letter *R*."

"'Pro'?" said Morgan. "Short for professional? Does that mean anything to anyone?"

"It could be an abbreviation," said Theo. "Like FBI stands for Federal Bureau of Investigations."

Harper tried to puzzle it out. "PRO could stand for all sorts of things. Or it could be POR, OPR . . ."

Morgan groaned. **"THIS IS IMPOSSIBLE."**

"Not impossible," said Harper. "But we need to do some studying." She smiled. **"WHO'S UP FOR A LITTLE RESEARCH IN THE LIBRARY TOMORROW?"**

Chapter 7

TIME TO HIT THE BOOKS! BUT NOT LITERALLY, BECAUSE THAT WOULD BE RUDE.

The next day after school, **Morgan and his friends gathered at the Stonesword Library, as they often did.**

But this time, they didn't head right for the computers and VR goggles. Morgan went to the information desk instead.

"Hi, Mr. Mallory," he said, greeting the media specialist. "What sorts of books do you have on codes and ciphers?"

Instead of answering him, Mr. Mallory tapped on the desk.

"Uh," said Morgan. **"Mr. Mallory, did you hear me?"**

The media specialist broke into a grin. "I guess you don't know Morse code," he said. "I just tapped out an answer to your question: we have *many* books on that topic. Come on, follow me!"

Within a few minutes, Morgan had joined Harper, Po, and Jodi in a small conference room **to work through the stack of books Mr. Mallory had pulled for them.** Harper was using her smartphone to search for online resources, too.

"This is a lot to wrap our heads around," said Po, rubbing his temple.

"I'll admit, I wish Theo were here," said Morgan. "He's good with brainteasers."

"I hope he's good at gardening, too," said Jodi. "I saw him with Ms. Minerva's landscaping club when I was walking here."

"Oh!" said Harper as her phone chimed. **"Ash is calling me back.** Hang on. . . ."

Harper set her phone up against a stack of books. Ash's face appeared on the screen, and she waved in greeting

"Hi, team!" she said. "Harper filled me in earlier. **I'm here to help any way I can."**

Morgan could feel himself growing calmer. Ash usually had that effect. Morgan liked to think of himself as the team's leader, but that wasn't always an easy thing to be. He had long ago realized that Ash was a natural problem solver. She also had a calm, confident energy that made challenges seem less overwhelming.

Jodi held the library's hamster up to the screen. **"Say hello to Duchess Dimples, Ash!"**

Ash bowed. "It's an honor to see you again, my duchess."

The hamster squeaked with pleasure.

"Okay, Ash," said Harper. "We've started in on all the books at Stonesword.

Do you want focus on abbreviations?"

"I still think the answer could be 'Please reheat oatmeal,'" said Po.

Morgan sighed. "I put it on the list, but I have a lot of doubt about it."

"I'm on it," said Ash. "And actually . . . what do you guys think if I ask some of my fellow scouts to help?"

Morgan's cheeks prickled. "I don't know about that," he said, without even really stopping to think about it first.

Harper peered at him over his open book. **"Why not?"** she asked. "If we're looking for an abbreviation, we're talking about thousands of possibilities. The more people sharing ideas, the faster it will go."

"Yeah," Morgan said. "I know. It's just . . ."

"Morgan doesn't like to share his toys," said Jodi. "He's always been that way."

Morgan scowled. "Only because my little sister used to *break* every toy she *borrowed*."

"I understand where you're coming from, Morgan," Harper said. "After all, we haven't told anyone about Doc's VR goggles. People think we're just playing regular Minecraft every day, not transporting to a virtual world where we're trying to rescue a broken artificial intelligence."

Po laughed. "I'm not sure people would believe us if *did* tell them."

"Harper's right," said Morgan. **"I like keeping the secret of the goggles to ourselves.** And I like having a club that feels special and is just ours. Remember, I wasn't very welcoming to Ash or to Theo."

"And look how that turned out," Jodi said. "It feels like they've *always* been part of the team."

Morgan thought about it for a long moment.

"Okay," he said at last. **"We need more people working on this puzzle.** Just . . . don't tell them more than they need to know, okay?"

"Got it," said Ash. "Thanks, Morgan. I'll hang up now and get to work."

After that, they returned to their books, poring over the pages for any hint at how to translate the bees' message. Twenty minutes passed in silence before Mr. Mallory appeared in the doorway.

"I found another book," he said. "Although I feel bad interrupting. **look at this hive mind at work!"**

"Hive mind?" said Po. "What does that mean?"

"I was just pointing out how well you were all working together," said Mr. Mallory. "A hive mind is a phenomenon you see in social insects, like the bees we're keeping here on the library grounds. It refers to the idea that every individual insect is doing its own thing . . . but they're all contributing to the good of the colony. **Almost like the bees were little parts of a single organism— like how your bodies are made up of lots and lots of little cells."**

Morgan had a thought. "Mr. Mallory?" he said. "What would happen if most of the colony wasn't there anymore?"

Mr. Mallory thought about it. "Well, if there weren't enough bees to perform all the tasks, then the colony would suffer. Perhaps it would be wiped out entirely." He shrugged. "But if there was still a queen bee to lay eggs, then the lost bees would be replaced. The new bees could take over for any bees that were lost, growing up to be either a drone or a worker."

A huge grin spread over Morgan's face. "Thanks, Mr. Mallory. That was a big help."

"It was?" said the media specialist. "Well, okay. **I'm not sure what hive minds have to do** with **codebreaking.**" He smiled. "But I do like it when kids are enthusiastic about learning. Maybe I should have been a teacher. . . ."

As Mr. Mallory departed, Morgan turned to his friends. "I think that's the answer," said Morgan. "I don't think there are enough bees left after the fire to give us the whole message." He snapped his fingers. **"They're probably spelling out what they were going to say before the lightning struck!"**

"We don't need to crack a code," Harper said with a sudden revelation. "We need to breed more Minecraft bees!"

"That's right," said Morgan. "Once the bee colony is large enough, every bee will contribute to the message." He looked at the clock. "I don't know if we have enough time to play today, but if we meet up tomorrow—"

Just then, Theo

came barging into the room looking for Harper. His nose was pink from the sun, and he wore thick gardening gloves. "You're still here," he said. "Thank goodness!"

"You're just in time, Theo," said Harper. "We've had a breakthrough."

"That'll have to wait," said Theo. "I was heading here from the school . . . and I walked past the beehive that Mr. Shane left behind, and—"

"What is it?" asked Harper.

"There's something wrong with the bees," said Theo. "They're sick. I think the bees are dying."

Chapter 8

ALAS, POOR BUZBY!
WE HARDLY KNEW YE.
(SNIFF.)

Harper knelt in the grass beside the beehive. Some of the bees seemed fine. They flew to and from the hive on their errands, buzzing as they went.

Other bees were obviously not well. They were having trouble flying. Harper saw one drop right out of the sky, and she went to pick up the little creature.

"Careful," warned Morgan. "You don't want to get stung."

"These gardening gloves are thick," said Theo. **"Here, Harper, use this extra pair."**

With one glove each, Harper and Theo worked

their way through the grass, lifting honeybees off the ground and placing them back atop the hive. "At least they won't be stepped on," said Harper. "But we still don't know what's causing the problem."

"Oh no!" said Jodi. **"It's too late for this one."** She cradled a bee in her palm. It was completely still, curled up in a little ball.

"Poor guy," said Po. **"We should give him a proper burial."**

"You all should set that up," said Harper. "I'm off to see a doctor."

Harper needed answers. And she knew only one place to go in order to get them.

"Doc!" she said, storming into the school lab. "Something's wrong with the bees."

At last, a bit of luck: Doc was still there, even though school had ended nearly an hour ago. **She looked up from an experiment in progress,** flipping her safety goggles up to her forehead. "Harper? What is it?"

Harper held out a gloved hand. She had a bee in her palm. The bee was alive but very still. It didn't try to fly away. It didn't try to do anything at all.

"This one dropped right out of the sky," she said. **"The same thing happened to several of them. One of them died."**

"Bring it here," said Doc. "Let's take a closer look."

Doc rummaged through her drawers until she found a device Harper had never seen before. **It looked almost like a microscope, but instead of sitting on a table, it fit over Doc's face.** She watched as Doc fiddled with the settings. "Place the bee on my desk," she said, and Harper did as she was told.

Doc leaned over the bee. The device whirred and clicked. **"This is a magnification device of my own making,"** she said. "Handy when examining anything smaller than a salamander but too big for a microscope."

"What are you looking for?" asked Harper.

"Parasites," answered Doc. "It's a common problem for bees. Little red mites will affix themselves to the bee's body and suck it dry." She shook her head. "I don't see any sign of them on this one, however."

She looked at Harper. **Her eye looked huge through the magnification lenses.**

"There must be some other problem," Doc said. "I'll take a look at the hive and see what I can find."

"I'm coming with you," said Harper.

→

While Doc examined the beehive, Jodi approached Harper with a matchbox. "Buzby is in here," said Jodi. "Theo is digging a little hole for him, and Morgan is going to give the eulogy."

Morgan's eyes went wide. **"I am? But I didn't**

even know him!"

"Morgan!" Po said in a scolding tone. "Don't speak ill of the dead."

Morgan tugged at his collar. "I guess I could come up with something nice to say."

Theo was on his knees, using his garden trowel to dig up dirt at the base of a tree.

"This is a nice spot, Theo," said Harper. "Good choice."

Theo nodded, then wiped the sweat from his brow. "That should be deep enough," he said.

Jodi carefully lowered the box into the hole. "Go ahead, Morgan," she said.

"Uh, we gather here today to pay our respects to a fallen honeybee," said Morgan. "I used to be afraid of bees, but now I know they aren't so scary. And since he was a drone, Buzby didn't even have a stinger. So . . . I guess he was all right, in my book."

"He just wanted to hang out at home and eat honey," said Po. "I totally get that."

They all stood in silence, looking down at the little box in the hole. Theo lifted his trowel. "Anything else?" he asked. "Or should I fill the hole now?"

"I have something to say," said Harper. She put her hands over her heart and closed her eyes. "I'm sorry this happened to you, Buzby. I'm sorry that the world wasn't a safer place for you."

"We're all sorry, Buzby," said Jodi.

"But we're going to do something about it," promised Harper. "We're going to figure out what happened to you. And we're going to save the rest of your colony. No matter what it takes."

Chapter 9

LET'S GIVE NATURE A HAND. . . . AFTER ALL, NATURE GAVE US HANDS TO START WITH!

There was nothing more they could do for the Stonesword bees. Doc needed time to run tests, but she promised to tell Harper as soon as she'd learned anything.

In the meantime, **the kids had a flower forest biome to rebuild.** Their saplings had already grown into adult trees, but the Minecraft bees wouldn't multiply on their own.

"Okay, Morgan," said Harper. "You're the expert. How do we breed bees?"

"It's easy," Morgan answered. **"TO START, WE JUST NEED FLOWERS."**

"Oh!" said Po, who was dressed as a giant

flower. "It's so nice to be needed."

Theo rolled his eyes. "You won't be so happy when the bees mistake you for lunch," he said.

"IT'S WORKING!" said Jodi, and she ran past them, laughing. She held a purple allium flower in her hand, and a bee was following her wherever she went.

"We don't know how many bees we'll need in order to receive their message," said Morgan. "But let's assume it's a big number. We'll want a lot of flowers."

"WE CAN EXPLORE THE NEARBY BIOMES," said Harper. "We'll gather whatever flowers we find and bring them back here."

"Even better if we find some bone meal," said Theo. "That will encourage new flowers to grow."

"PICKING FIGHTS WITH SKELETONS?" said Po. "Who knew that raising bees would be so adventurous?"

The work went quickly once everyone had their assignments. Jodi in particular enjoyed the task of finding various flowers, and Theo liked replanting them in the flower forest. Morgan proved adept at flushing skeletons out of caves and leading them into an ambush. Po especially liked defeating the undead mobs while dressed as a flower.

Harper took on the task of breeding more bees. She would wait until Jodi and Theo had an extra flower to spare, then she would feed the flower to the nearest bee. Soon, several little baby bees fluttered through the forest.

"They need a place to live," Harper said of the baby bees. "There's no room for them in the nest."

"I've got an idea for that," said Morgan. **"BUT WE NEED HONEYCOMB FIRST."**

Morgan showed Harper how the Minecraft bees acted much like their real-world counterparts. "Watch," he said. "The bees will fly to a flower to collect nectar. Then they'll return to their nest to make honey with it."

Harper noticed that little flecks of yellow stuck to the bees' bodies when they interacted with a flower. **"IS THAT POLLEN?"** she asked.

"Yeah," said Morgan. "Again, it's just like real life. The bees get pollen on them, and the pollen spreads all over the forest. It can make some plants grow faster. Crops and berry bushes, for instance."

"We should plant some berry bushes," Harper suggested. "I think they'd look nice in our forest."

Sometime later, after the sun had gone down, Harper saw what Morgan had been waiting for. "Look," she said. **"THEIR NEST IS DRIPPING WITH HONEY."**

"We'll have to be careful with this next part," he said. "Since it's night, the bees are inside their nest, and we don't want to upset them. Get your shears ready. But don't use them until I say."

Harper watched as Morgan lit a campfire beneath the honey-heavy nest. **"SMOKE FROM THE FIRE WILL KEEP THE BEES CALM,"** he said. "Now you can use the shears on the nest to cut away some honeycomb."

Harper did just as he said. With a quick snip, several pieces of honeycomb fell into her inventory.

"Perfect," said Morgan. "With honeycomb and wood, we can make beehives, which means the new bees will have a place to live, and— Look out!"

Harper whirled around just in time to see a zombie lurching toward her. She ducked out of the path of its attack.

MISSING HER, THE ZOMBIE STRUCK A NEARBY BEE INSTEAD.

"Hey, watch it!" said Harper, and she drew her sword to defend the insect.

But to her surprise, the bee could take care of itself. It dove at the zombie, flipping around and striking the undead mob with its stinger. **The zombie flared red as it took damage.**

"Ooh, that looked like it hurt," said Harper.

"Only a little bit," said Morgan. "Normally, a bee will poison whatever it stings. But poison doesn't work on zombies."

"Then I'd better help it out," Harper said. With the zombie focused on the bee, **Harper easily finished off the undead mob with her sword.**

"Did you see that, Morgan?" Harper said. "That bee and I make a good team!"

But when she turned around, she saw Morgan

gazing at the bee. **"IT LOST ITS STINGER WHEN IT ATTACKED THE ZOMBIE,"** he said. **"IT CAN'T SURVIVE FOR LONG WITHOUT IT."**

And true to Morgan's word, the bee dropped moments later, disappearing in a cloud of dust.

"No!" said Harper. "Not when we were finally making progress!"

"I guess it's an important lesson," Morgan said. **"THESE BEES NEED TO BE PROTECTED, JUST LIKE THEIR REAL-WORLD COUSINS."**

Morgan held out a plank of wood and asked, "Do you have that honeycomb? We should get these bees a new home before there's any more trouble."

Chapter 10

HONEYBEES DON'T GET WEEKENDS OFF, BUT THEY DON'T GET POP QUIZZES, EITHER!

In the real world, it was the weekend, and Harper and her friends had decided to go on a fact-finding mission.

Harper's parents were more than a little confused by her request. "Are you sure you want to go to the orchard *today*?" they asked. "Apple-picking season is weeks away."

"That's *why* I want to go today," said Harper. "I'm not interested in the apples. I'm interested in the bees that are *pollinating* the apple blossoms."

In the end, they'd agreed, and they dropped Harper off at the orchard while they ran errands nearby.

Her friends were there waiting, and they'd already found Mr. Shane. **The man had traded his cowboy attire for a beekeeper suit.** He had taken the beehives off his truck and set them all over the orchard grounds. When Harper arrived, he had just removed a tray from one of the hives, and he was scraping fresh honey off of the tray and into a glass bottle. **Bees were crawling all over him, but he didn't seem to mind.**

Po frowned at the sight, though. "I'd go up and say hi," he said, "but even if bees aren't aggressive, I don't want to be outnumbered a hundred to one."

"I'll do it," said Harper, and she strode forward, waving her arms. "Hi!" she said. "Sorry! Mr. Shane? It's important!"

Theo grinned. "I guess she means business."

"She made a promise on Buzby's grave," Jodi reminded him. "Nothing's more serious than that."

Mr. Shane held up a hand to keep Harper from coming too close. He put the hive back together, grabbed the bottle of honey, and came toward them. "Can I help you?"

"We're hoping that *we* can help *you*, actually," Harper said. "Your bees are in trouble. The ones you left by the school, I mean. And we're trying to find out why."

Mr. Shane came closer, removing his helmet. The skin around his eyes crinkled as he smiled at them. "You must be Doc Culpepper's students," he said. "She called me about the problem. I'll tell you what I told her: it's sadly pretty common, these days." He sighed. "I lose a lot of bees."

"Why?" asked Harper. **"Why do honeybees need so much help to survive?"**

Mr. Shane tipped his head at her. "I'm happy to tell you more," he said. "But let's walk while we talk."

Harper had been to the orchard before, but never when the trees were in full bloom. It was a beautiful sight. "I didn't realize apple blossoms were so pretty," she said.

"They're pretty . . . and they're an important part of the natural balance," he said. "I'm sure Doc's told you all about how this works. Bees seek out flowers for nectar to eat. That's where honey comes from. But while the bees are getting what they need from the flowers . . . the flowers are getting what *they* need from the bees. The insects spread pollen from the flowers all around. Then the flowers become fruit, and the seeds from the fruit ensure that more trees grow." He patted a nearby tree trunk. "It's a pretty good system. Worked well for millions of years. Then people came along, and things got complicated."

Po crunched loudly into an apple.

"Oh," said Po. "Sorry! I didn't think that was going to be so noisy."

"Where did you even get that?" asked Theo. "There aren't any apples here yet!"

"It's from the grocery store," said Po.

"Aha!" said Mr. Shane. "See, that's interesting. We know it isn't apple season around here. The bees are only now doing the work of pollinating. But it's apple season somewhere—in another climate, maybe another hemisphere. And people have gotten used to having year-round access to every kind of fruit and vegetable you can imagine."

"Thafsa good fing," Po said around a mouthful of apple.

"It's not a bad thing—not always," agreed Mr.

Shane. "Believe me, I'm happy to have year-round access to avocados. But sometimes we put our own needs and our convenience ahead of the needs of the planet." **He shook his head.** "Truth is, this orchard shouldn't need an old cowboy coming through with a truck full of bees. The bees should be in this area year-round; they should find the orchard without my help. But we've got the environment all mixed up. You see this patch of wild growth over here?"

Mr. Shane had led them to the edge of the orchard, where tall grasses, weeds, and wildflowers grew in a tangle.

"What a mess!" said Theo, and he pulled out his garden trowel. "You want me to clean this up? **I'm getting good at landscaping."**

"You're proving my point for me, son," said Mr. Shane. "You think this looks chaotic. You think it needs to be fixed. **But this is nature!** And this is what bees need to survive." He clucked his tongue. "This town's perfect lawns might look nice in a picture, but bees starve without the tangled growth and bountiful flowers. And all the

herbicides, fungicides, and pesticides are murder
on the poor fellows. Literally."

"P-pesticides?" said Theo. "Pesticides hurt
the bees?"

"Naturally," said Mr. Shane. "Gardeners will
spray poison to keep pests away. But poison hurts
all sorts of creatures, not just the pests."

Harper watched as Theo went pale before her
very eyes.

"What's wrong, Theo?" she asked.

"Woodsword's landscaping club," he said. "We

use that stuff. Herbicides, fungicides, pesticides . . . we were trying to fix up Woodsword's lawn, to make it look *better*."

"Dude," said Po. "Stonesword is right across the street from the school. **All it would take is a breeze, and those chemicals would spread to the library.**"

"And I'm sure the bees can't resist crossing the street to visit the school's plants," Harper added.

"I've seen them," said Jodi. "They were buzzing right outside the window during homeroom yesterday."

"It's my fault, isn't it?" said Theo. **My new club is killing the bees!**"

Chapter 11

CLASH OF THE TEACHERS—
OR JUST ANOTHER
EPIC SCHOOL DAY AT
WOODSWORD?!

"Let me talk to Ms. Minerva," said Theo. "I think she'll listen to me."

But he wasn't as confident as he tried to sound.

It was early Monday morning, and Harper and Theo had arrived early at school. Their mission was simple: **they had to convince Ms. Minerva to stop using harsh chemicals on Woodsword's lawn.**

It did not go as well as they had hoped.

"Can't you just move the bees?" asked Ms. Minerva.

"Well . . . ," said Theo, "I suppose . . ."

"We could move this particular hive," said

Harper. "But this is part of a bigger problem. **We want bees to thrive in this area.** It's better for the ecosystem if they do."

"*Not* if it means letting the schoolyard become overrun with weeds," said Ms. Minerva. "Nobody wants that. Your parents would be the first to write angry letters. A school needs to look presentable."

"But at what cost?" asked Harper. "Here, Ms. Minerva. I got this for you."

She handed the teacher an apple blossom.

"A flower? I don't understand."

"There's a tradition where students give teachers a bright, shiny apple. But an apple at this time of year would have to be shipped in from another country on a carbon-emitting plane or boat. And for the apple to be perfectly bright and shiny, that probably means the farmers used chemicals, and threw away anything with a blemish." **Harper shrugged.** "Maybe we should be happy with what we have."

"Hear, hear," said a voice from the doorway. Harper turned to see Doc. "I couldn't agree more,

Harper. And I'm eager to see what changes will be made to the landscaping club."

"Hold on," said Ms. Minerva. **"I haven't agreed to anything yet."**

"After such an impassioned speech?" said Doc. "If you'd been there for Buzby's funeral, you wouldn't be so heartless."

"Who in the world is Buzby?" asked Ms. Minerva.

"A fallen friend," said Doc. **"He was poisoned**

by the landscaping club."

Minerva rolled her eyes, clearly thinking, *Now what?!* "My club isn't poisoning anybody."

"Well, not on *purpose*," said Theo.

"We've got a problem on our hands, Minerva," said Doc. "Fortunately, I've come up with some solutions."

"Oh, I can just imagine your solutions," said Ms. Minerva, and she squeezed the bridge of her nose. "A lot of sharp objects on wheels, roaming the school grounds?"

"I would phrase it as 'automated landscaping,'" argued Doc.

"I'd really prefer that you not replace my students with robots," said Ms. Minerva.

"It's your chemicals I want to replace," said Doc. "Listen, how sensitive is your nose? Because I've got a new fertilizer formula, but the result is *very* pungent. . . ."

Harper tried a few times to get a word in. But the teachers were firmly locked in their debate, with Doc pushing for the landscaping club to change the way it worked to something greener . . . **and possibly more technologically robust.** But she pushed too hard, relying on science that Ms. Minerva simply didn't trust.

When Harper and Theo finally slipped out of the classroom, the teachers didn't even seem to notice they were leaving.

Chapter 12

A SPELLING BEE TO REMEMBER! IF ANYONE (INCLUDING THE BEES) GETS OUT ALIVE . . .

Harper took comfort in the fact that things were going better in Minecraft than they'd been going at school.

"THIS IS IT!" said Jodi. She held up a bright blue cornflower. "This is the last flower we needed for our forest restoration project. Now we've got at least one of everything."

"Except blue orchids," said Theo. "They only grow in swamps, so they would be out of place here."

"SAME WITH SUNFLOWERS," said Morgan.

"Oh, and we didn't include Wither roses," added Theo. "For obvious reasons."

Jodi squinted her virtual eyes. "You guys are so *technical.* The point is, we're done gathering flowers. AND THEO AND I CAME UP WITH A DESIGN TO MAKE SURE OUR FLOWER FOREST IS AS BEAUTIFUL AS POSSIBLE."

Theo grinned. "We were inspired by the orchard, actually. All those perfect rows of planted trees. We wanted our forest to feel organized." He turned to Harper. "I think you'll like what we've done so far."

But when Harper saw the state of the forest, **she didn't like it one bit.**

"It's . . . nice," she said.

But she couldn't fool Theo.

"What?" he said. "WHAT'S WRONG?!"

Harper gazed out at the field of flowers, all organized by color and arranged in artful rows. It actually *did* look nice. But it didn't look like a flower forest biome. It looked like a garden rather than a natural space.

"I think we're worried too much about how it looks," suggested Harper. "WE SHOULD BE THINKING ABOUT WHAT THE BEES NEED."

"SHE'S GOT A POINT," said Morgan. "The bees will only leave their hives if there are flowers nearby. We should move some of these flowers, to make sure that happens."

Theo slapped his forehead. "I'm doing it again, aren't I? It's the same mistake I made in the real world!" He shook his head. "I just like symmetry. And order. I like things to be neat and to make sense."

"I know," said Harper. "And that's a really good thing when you're programming or doing a research project. Or cleaning your room!" She put her arm around him. **"BUT NATURE DOESN'T MIND A LITTLE CLUTTER. AND WE SHOULD LEARN TO BE OKAY WITH THAT."**

Theo sighed. "Technically, this isn't nature. It's a randomized digitally generated re-creation." Harper started to react, but he smirked good-naturedly and quickly added, "Still, I know what you mean."

"I don't know what *anybody* is talking about," said Jodi. "Just keep the yellow flowers close to the purple flowers, okay? They're complementary!"

With the final flowers in place, the forest was alive again. **Harper saw chickens, a rabbit . . . and bees.**

They'd successfully bred and created homes for a great number of bees.

"There they go," she said. "That one is making a *P* again. And an *R* . . . *O* . . . *T* . . ."

"Eep, hold on!" said Jodi. "There's a spider over there! Two of them, in fact."

Harper turned to look. Jodi was right. Two spiders skittered beneath nearby trees.

"It should be fine," said Theo. **"IT'S LIGHT OUT, SO THEY WON'T BE HOSTILE."**

"But that will change when the sun goes down," said Morgan. "And if they get into a fight with the bees, we might have to start all over again."

"Jodi and I can take care of the spiders," said Po. "Easy. And to be honest, I'd rather do that than play Spelling Bee."

"Okay," Morgan said reluctantly. "But holler if you need help."

"You know me," said Po, and he drew his sword. "I scream really good when I'm in trouble."

"And sometimes when he isn't!" said Jodi, running after him.

Harper kept one eye on her friends and one eye on the bees. There was an *E* . . . and a *C* . . .

"They're telling us to protect someone," said Harper. "Or something."

"Check this out!" said Po, and **he pelted a spider with arrows.**

"Uh, we might need some help, actually," said Jodi. "There are . . . sort of a lot of . . ."

"I got this," Morgan said. "Spiders are so easy." He leapt into battle, swinging his sword.

"Should we help?" asked Theo.

"You go ahead," said Harper. **"I'LL SEE WHAT THE BEES HAVE TO SAY."**

"PROTECT THE . . . SOMETHING," said
Theo. "Let me know!" And he joined
the fray.

Harper spared a quick
glance. There really were
a lot of spiders all of a
sudden. Where were they
all coming from?

Fortunately, her friends were equal to the task. **The spiders didn't get anywhere close to the bees.** And the bees, one after another, performed their dance for Harper.

In the end, the wording of their message was clear, even if the meaning was not.

"PROTECT THE BALANCE," Harper said after the last bee had completed its movement. "Protect *what* balance?"

Before Harper could puzzle out the meaning, an alarming change came over the assembled bees.

Their eyes turned red.

Their buzzing grew more intense.

Some of them turned their stingers in her direction.

"Hey, everyone!" she yelled. "We have a problem here."

"Sort of busy!" Po shouted back.

And Harper realized she was trapped between hostile spiders on one side . . .

. . . and angry bees on the other **. . . and both were closing in on her fast!**

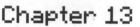

Chapter 13

ANGRY BEES TO THE LEFT OF ME! SPIDERS TO THE RIGHT! (BUT AT LEAST THERE'S GOOD SYMMETRY!)

Harper ran to rejoin her friends as quickly as she could.

It wasn't fast enough to avoid being stung in the back.

"OW!" she cried, and she felt the bee's poison weakening her. Worse, she knew that the bee that had stung her would die.

She didn't want that to happen. She didn't want to fight the bees. **She'd just spent days bringing them back from the brink of disaster!**

"What did you do?" asked Morgan.

"Nothing!" said Harper. She held up her shield,

blocking a dive-bombing bee. "They delivered their message, and then they got really mad."

Morgan swatted the nearest bee away with his hand, clearly afraid that a sword would do too much damage. "What was the message?" he asked.

"Protect the balance," Harper said. **"ARE THEY MAD BECAUSE WE AREN'T DOING THAT?"**

"Uh," said Po, also swatting a bee. "Jodi and I did sort of cause a forest fire."

"We're very sorry about it!" said Jodi as she ran in circles, pursued by angry bees.

"But we fixed that damage," said Theo. "We restored the balance. They should have forgiven us for that." As he focused on dodging a bee, a spider struck him from behind. "Yowch! Okay, this is ridiculous. *Where* are the spiders coming from?"

"I THINK THEY'RE COMING OUT OF THAT HOLE!" said Jodi, motioning over her shoulder as she ran past. "Over that way!"

Theo and Harper fought their way through the spiders, working in the direction Jodi had indicated. They found the hole, and inside it . . .

"A dungeon," said Theo. **"WE MUST HAVE**

MADE THIS HOLE BY ACCIDENT WHEN WE WERE LANDSCAPING."

"And there's a spawner inside," said Harper. She could see the glow of its fire, flickering in the dark. The spawner would keep making spiders as long as they could defeat them.

"I'VE GOT TO DESTROY IT," Theo said. "That'll take care of the spiders, at least." He traded his sword for a pickaxe and carved a bigger hole, giving him easy access to the spawner.

He raised his pickaxe, ready to destroy it.

And Harper yelled, **"STOP!"**

Theo did stop, but his confusion was obvious. "Why am I stopping?" he asked, holding his pickaxe just above the spider spawner.

"The bees' message," Harper said. "The balance. **WE'RE DISRUPTING THE BALANCE!** We had no right to attack the spiders like we did. We started the fight. Just like we started the fire."

"So what can we do about it now?" asked Theo.

"We can leave," said Harper. "We put this biome back together. Now we should . . . just leave it be."

Theo trusted Harper, but Morgan wasn't happy with

the plan. "It feels like we're retreating," he said. "Like we're giving up."

Then another stingerless bee fell at his feet, and he reconsidered. "But it's obvious that we're causing harm to the bees all over again." He sighed. "Okay. Let's get out of here."

Harper and her friends fled the forest as quickly as they could. The spiders soon gave up the chase, dropping their hostility and returning to their business. The bees, however, pursued the group to the very edge of the forest.

"MAYBE THEY WON'T FOLLOW US INTO THE TAIGA," said Po.

But as they watched, the bees flew above the trees of the flower forest in a great black swarm.

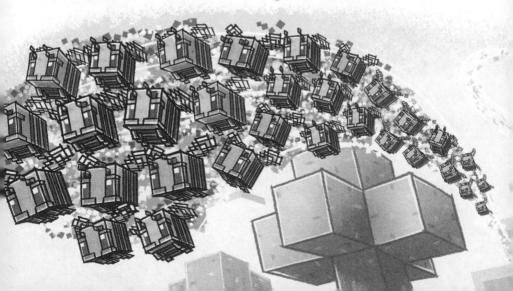

They roiled and rippled like a dark cloud before descending. The swarm was aiming directly for the kids.

Harper hefted her shield, ready for another fight. . . .

But the swarm didn't attack. The bees moved in an intricate dance, once more positioning themselves into a shape that looked humanoid. The buzzing noise of their wings grew louder, and then harmonized.

The buzzing once more sounded like a voice.

"Zzank youz . . . ," it said. *"For rezztoring zee balance. Rezzpecting. Protect-zing."*

Harper stepped forward. She tried to look the

being in its eyes, but it didn't have any. Or rather, it had too many. **The eyes of dozens of bees all looked back at her.**

"You're . . . you're welcome," she said. "We'll be more careful in the future. We care about this place."

"WE WANT TO FIX THE FAULT!" Theo added, stepping forward. "Please. **CAN YOU HELP US?"**

"*Findz. Findz . . . golem,*" said the bees. "*Findzzz*

golem . . . or elzzzzze."

Their message delivered, the buzzing bees fused together in a flash of light . . . to form the missing arm of the Evoker King.

A kaleidoscope of butterflies lowered the piece of her friend gently into Harper's outstretched hands. They dispersed as soon as she gripped it.

Chapter 14

ALL'S WELL THAT ENDS WELL ... EXCEPT FOR THAT BIG HOLE IN THE SKY.

A few days later, Harper wore her new T-shirt to an afterschool ceremony. As the newest member of the **Woodsword Gardening and Landscaping Club,** she wanted to show off her club pride.

"Thank you all for coming," said Shelly Silver. She stood before Woodsword's new garden. Harper hoped it would be the first of many.

Shelly continued, "As class president, it's my honor to preside over the grand opening of the school's first wild garden. Free of chemicals, the plants and flowers within this garden will be allowed to grow naturally—**and will still give**

our gardening club an opportunity to work their green thumbs. It's only the start of a plan for expanding greener practices to all of Woodsword."

"We've chosen plants that are native to the area," added Ms. Minerva. "And the gardening and landscaping club is committing to pulling harmful weeds by hand—*without* resorting to chemicals . . . or robots." She smiled. "But Doc Culpepper did provide some wonderful ideas for improving the nutrients in our soil. So I guess it's fair to say she and I have buried the hatchet . . . just as we've buried some flower bulbs that will bloom next spring!"

The crowd cheered as Ms. Minerva used a pair of garden shears to cut the ribbon around the garden. The teacher smiled, and Harper understood why. Even though the garden was wild, it was well maintained. Instead of using harsh chemicals to make the garden look "nice," Theo and the rest of the club had promised to use elbow grease. **Pulling weeds the old-fashioned way would take the work of many hands.**

That was why Harper had agreed to sign up. **And it was why she gave Theo a big hug, right there in front of the garden.**

"Thank you for convincing Ms. Minerva to try this," she said. "I know she won't regret it."

Theo blushed. "*I* definitely don't regret it."

"However," said Harper, and she took the gardening shears from Ms. Minerva. **"I do have some ideas about how to make our equipment more efficient.** I bet Doc has some digital technology that could really make these shears work wonders."

Ms. Minerva ran her hands through her hair. "Let's not go overboard, now, Harper."

Doc herself was just across the street, helping Mr. Shane retrieve the Stonesword hive. She called Harper over to say goodbye.

"I'll be back again, same time next year," said Mr. Shane. "In the meantime, enjoy some local apples and think of my bees, all right?"

"We will," promised Harper. **"I'm just sad the bees can't stay behind."**

"Well, speaking of that," said Mr. Shane. "You and your friends did such a good job taking care of them that I thought I'd leave you with a present. I can't leave a whole hive behind, of course . . ." **Mr. Shane handed Doc a tray from the hive.** It had several bees crawling on it. "But I can leave you with a few bees, including a brand-new queen. It's enough to start a colony of your very own."

Harper gasped with delight. **"We'll take good care of them,"** she promised.

"The whole landscaping club can work together to keep them happy and safe," said Theo. "They'll have all the flowers they could want."

"That's what I like to hear," said

Mr. Shane, and once he was done loading up his truck, he stepped into the cab. The tarp had been tied firmly in place, and **Harper knew the bees beneath it were off to their next adventure.**

But she had plenty of adventure to look forward to right here at home. And she was glad that the bees—some of them, at least—were here to stay.

In Minecraft, however, Harper's happy ending was soon forgotten in the face of a very large hole in the sky.

"**THE FAULT'S GOTTEN EVEN BIGGER,**" she said. "I didn't think it was possible."

"I worry about what will happen when it fills the sky," Theo said, looking across the Overworld. "Will it spread to the ground beneath our feet?"

"It won't come to that," said Morgan. "**WE'LL FIND A WAY.**"

"I believe you, Morgan," said Po, and he pointed. "Because I just saw a butterfly heading that way."

"Already?" said Jodi. "We're in luck!"

They all moved together as a group, pursuing the butterfly through a cluster of trees.

On the other side, a mass of the insects fluttered their colorful wings. **They were all flying around a familiar object.**

"So much for luck," said Harper. **"THAT'S A PORTAL TO THE NETHER."**

"I guess we know where we'll find **THE GOLEM**," said Morgan. **"READY . . . OR NOT."**

MINECRAFT
WOODSWORD CHRONICLES

Based on the most popular video game of all time, this all-new chapter book series takes a group of intrepid Minecraft players deeper into the game than ever before!

INTO THE GAME!

Five young Minecraft players in the real world find themselves transported inside the game they love. But now it's not a game—and they will have to use everything they know to explore, build, and survive!

978-1-9848-5045-4 (trade) — 978-1-9848-5047-8 (ebook) —
978-0-593-40120-0 (digital audio) — 978-1-9848-5046-1 (lib. bdg.)

NIGHT OF THE BATS!

When zombie hordes attack them in the game and bats invade their school in the real world, Ash, Morgan, and their friends realize that it's going to take all their talents to get to the bottom of these monstrous migrations.

978-1-9848-5048-5 (trade) — 978-1-9848-5050-8 (ebook) —
978-0-593-40123-1 (digital audio) — 978-1-9848-5049-2 (lib. bdg.)

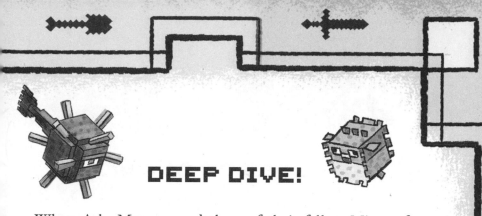

DEEP DIVE!

When Ash, Morgan, and three of their fellow Minecraft players, who can actually enter the game, take a deep dive into the Aquatic biome, they find a world filled with beauty and wonder. A treasure map promises adventure and the opportunity to explore—but it could also be a trap set by the mysterious Evoker King.

978-1-9848-5051-5 (trade) — 978-1-9848-5053-9 (ebook) — 978-0-593-40124-8 (digital audio) — 978-1-9848-5052-2 (lib. bdg.)

GHAST IN THE MACHINE!

Jodi, Ash, Morgan, and their fellow Minecraft players go out into the real world to find clues to the identity of the mysterious and sinister Evoker King. Not only do they need to find out who—or what—he is, but they need to know if it's really possible for him to escape the game!

978-1-9848-5062-1 (trade) — 978-1-9848-5064-5 (ebook) — 978-0-593-40126-2 (digital audio) — 978-1-9848-5063-8 (lib. bdg.)

DUNGEON CRAWL!

When Po, Morgan, and three of their fellow Minecraft players track the Evoker King to his home in the heart of a perilous dungeon, they have to gear up for an epic fantasy quest filled with danger, dragons, and hostile mobs.

978-1-9848-5065-2 (trade) — 978-1-9848-5067-6 (ebook) — 978-0-593-40128-6 (digital audio) — 978-1-9848-5066-9 (lib. bdg.)

LAST BLOCK STANDING!

As the world of Minecraft falls under the Evoker King's control, Morgan, Ash, and their friends get ready for the final showdown. But with their enemy now in possession of the most powerful building block in Minecraft, do they really stand a chance of defeating him?

978-1-9848-5069-0 (trade) — 978-1-9848-5071-3 (ebook) — 978-0-593-40130-9 (digital audio) — 978-1-9848-5070-6 (lib. bdg.)

THE ADVENTURES CONTINUE IN

MINECRAFT STONESWORD SAGA

CRACK IN THE CODE!

Someone—or something—has turned the Evoker King to stone. And now a new player, Theo, has joined the team on their quest to return their former enemy to normal. Theo has modding skills that could come in handy, but does he have what it takes to be part of the team, or will his meddling put a crack in the game code that none of them will survive?

978-0-593-37298-2 (trade) — 978-0-593-37300-2 (ebook) —
978-0-593-40132-3 (digital audio) — 978-0-593-37299-9 (lib. bdg.)

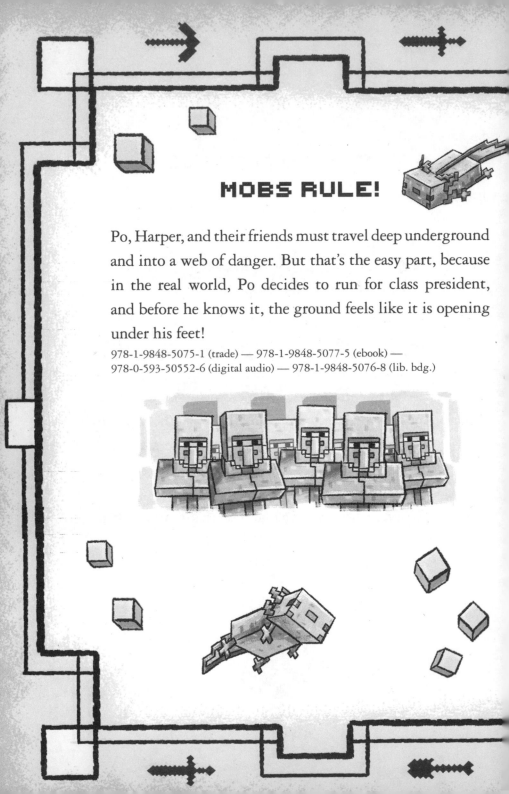

MOBS RULE!

Po, Harper, and their friends must travel deep underground and into a web of danger. But that's the easy part, because in the real world, Po decides to run for class president, and before he knows it, the ground feels like it is opening under his feet!

978-1-9848-5075-1 (trade) — 978-1-9848-5077-5 (ebook) — 978-0-593-50552-6 (digital audio) — 978-1-9848-5076-8 (lib. bdg.)

NEW PETS ON THE BLOCK!

When the third piece of the Evoker King takes the form of a Minecraft witch and sends Jodi, Morgan, and their friends on a quest to bring back an extremely rare animal mob, Jodi is determined to make sure that the mob stays safe no matter what!

978-1-9848-5094-2 (trade) — 978-1-9848-5096-6 (ebook) — 978-0-593-55978-9 (digital audio) — 978-1-9848-5095-9 (lib. bdg.)

MINECRAFT is a game about placing blocks and going on adventures. Build, play, and explore across infinitely generated worlds of mountains, caverns, oceans, jungles, and deserts. Defeat hordes of zombies, bake the cake of your dreams, venture to new dimensions, or build a skyscraper. What you do in Minecraft is up to you.

Nick Eliopulos is a writer who lives in Brooklyn (as many writers do). He likes to spend half his free time reading and the other half gaming. He cowrote the Adventurers Guild series with his best friend and works as a narrative designer for a small video game studio. After all these years, Endermen still give him the creeps.

Alan Batson is a British cartoonist and illustrator. His works include *Everything I Need to Know I Learned from a Star Wars Little Golden Book, Everything That Glitters is Guy!,* and *Spider-Ham.* Being extremely fond of cubes and travel to exotic places, he has recently begun to lend his talents to several different books on adventures in the world of Minecraft.

Chris Hill is an illustrator living in Birmingham, England, with his wife and two daughters and has been loving it for twenty-five years! When he's not working, he spends time with his family and trying to tire out his dog on long walks. If there's any time left after that, he loves to go riding on his motorcycle, feeling the wind on his face while contemplating his next illustration adventure.

JOURNEY INTO THE WORLD OF

MINECRAFT

—BOOKS FOR EVERY READING LEVEL—

OFFICIAL NOVELS:

FOR YOUNGER READERS:

OFFICIAL GUIDES:

DISCOVER MORE AT READMINECRAFT.COM

Penguin
Random
House